SUITCASE S(WITCH)

AISHA BUSHBY

Illustrated by
CORALIE MUCE

Barrington Stoke

First published in 2023 in Great Britain by
Barrington Stoke Ltd
18 Walker Street, Edinburgh, EH3 7LP

www.barringtonstoke.co.uk
A CIP catalogue record for this book is available
from the British Library upon request

ISBN: 978-1-80090-176-6

Printed by Hussar Books, Poland

CONTENTS

CHAPTER 1

The Accidental Switch

I love riding the train. I love the sound of the wheels chug-chug-chugging along the tracks. The feeling of the carriage swaying left and right. The fun of trying to walk up and down the carriage without toppling over.

But mostly I love the way the world outside blurs past in a haze of colour. It's like one of those landscape paintings you see in galleries, where trees are made of dozens of different shades of green.

I just wish there was a whistle that blew whenever the train slowed down and sped up,

like the old trains had. Instead, there's a robotic voice over the loudspeaker saying we've arrived at our weekend destination. A little town by the sea!

We don't often go away for the weekend, because Mum works a lot, but this weekend is extra special ... On Sunday I'm entering a SCARY competition.

Out of everyone in my year, I've been selected to read a series of poems I've written. If I win the competition, I'll get a £500 voucher for books for my school library, which is a BIG DEAL. But I'm going to have to read them in front of hundreds of people, which is terrifying. Here's the first one:

There once was a green crocodile,
Who swam the full length of the Nile,
While journeying back,
They met a great yak,
Who talked for a rather long while.

It's a limerick, which is a type of poem that comes from Ireland. They're meant to be funny and sometimes rude. Mine isn't rude, really, unless you count the insult to the yak. And personally, I like people who talk a lot.

I wrote a haiku too, which is a Japanese poem made up of three lines. The first line has five syllables, the second seven, and the third five again.

My third and final poem I'm supposed
to read out is an Italian sonnet, which is the
longest and most difficult to remember. The
theme for my collection is "Poems from around
the world", because that's like me, sort of.

"We're nearly there now, Zahra," Dad says.

I was hoping I'd be able to practise my
poems on the train, but I felt a little sick, so I
put my notebook in my suitcase to keep it safe
and spent most of the journey staring out of the
window and listening to music with Dad.

He puts his headphones away now, while
Mum slams her laptop shut. She promised she
would only work on the train journeys there and
back – it has taken four whole hours from where
we live in the Midlands. But I bet she'll sneak in
little bits of work when Dad and I are asleep.

I've never seen Mum sleep, and I have this
theory that she's actually a vampire, so she
doesn't need to. Mum is always awake when

I go to bed and when I get up in the morning. But she's not pale, like the vampires you read about.

Mum has brown skin which she inherited from her mum, who was from Kuwait. Mum also inherited other things, like a red cardigan she always wears and a pair of gold earrings in the shape of a leaf. She says they keep her connected to her past despite her mum being gone.

Dad has white skin and his mum is very much still around. He inherits lots of things from her all the time, including weekly homemade cakes and flowers from her garden. Unlike Mum, Dad likes to sleep in, so I know he's not a vampire.

I'm not sure what I inherited from my parents, but I hope I work hard like Mum when I'm grown up but still get to sleep as much as Dad does.

I wobble down the carriage towards the luggage rack to collect my suitcase, which is bright purple with orange polka dots on it. A girl about my age is coming from the other direction. She's wearing a witch's hat. It's not

Halloween but, looking at the rest of her outfit, she's definitely in some sort of fancy dress. Maybe she's going to a party?

The girl grins at me and takes her suitcase, which looks *exactly* the same as mine. Once the train has stopped, she turns elegantly, steps out of the open train doors and glides away. By saying "glides", I'm not just using a fancy word to describe the girl walking. I'm pretty sure she *actually* glided.

"Hurry up, Zee," Mum says, helping me with my suitcase. "Or the doors will shut and we'll be carted off to the next station!"

I got so distracted by the girl that I'm just standing there while everyone bumps around me. An old lady tuts until Mum glares at her, which makes the lady apologise. See? Vampire. Mum can make people do things too.

We make it off the train just as the doors start making that beep-beep-beep noise that

they do and slam shut. The train begins
chugging away to its next location.

*

The flat we're staying in is on the top floor of an
old building with creaky stairs and tall ceilings.
I can see the sea when I walk up to the window
in the living room.

There's a fire escape out the back – a metal
staircase that runs down from the window
of my bedroom all the way to the ground. It
creaks in the wind.

Dad tells me to unpack and hang up all of
my clothes before we go out for fish and chips
on the beach.

I do as he says and open my suitcase on the
floor of my bedroom. But I notice almost at
once that something is wrong. I can't see my
jeans, T-shirts, chequered shirts and trainers.

Instead, there are black dresses and striped trousers, purple velvet boots and a cloak.

I frown, wondering for a moment if I'd somehow packed all of these unfamiliar clothes without remembering.

But then I realise what must have happened, like a wave from the ocean has swept over me. I accidentally swapped suitcases with the witch!

CHAPTER 2

A Surprise Visit

"She's not a *real* witch," Mum says in her know-it-all way when I tell her about the suitcases.

"That's not really the point, Mum," I remind her. "What am I going to wear?" I shriek. This weekend is going to be a disaster!

"Hmm," Mum says, thinking about it. "We'll get you some clothes tomorrow, don't worry."

"And I'll wash the clothes you wore today when we get back," Dad says, "so you have something for the morning."

That solves my immediate problem, but I'm also a bit sad because I packed all of my favourite clothes for this weekend, including a super-special dress to wear to my poetry reading. And – OH NO! – I've just realised ALL of my poems are in my book, which is also in my suitcase.

I start crying softly on the floor, like a little kitten, with the witch's things all around me. I still can't believe we switched suitcases.

I decide to check the girl's suitcase in case there's a tag with her address on it. Before I know it, I'm looking inside. The first thing I notice is a leatherbound diary, hand-stitched, a maroon purple colour. The pages are made of really thick paper, and it has the feeling of being something really old and special.

I open it to the first page, and it says:

Property of Daria Foxglove

That must be the girl's name, but sadly there doesn't seem to be an address.

The inner pages are all laid out kind of like my homework diary at school, which has days of the week on the right where I'm meant to put down my homework deadlines and any school activities. And on the left is a blank page for making notes. My blank pages are full of doodles because I find it hard to just listen in lessons without doing something with my hands. Luckily, my teachers are really nice about it as they know it helps me concentrate.

Anyway, the pages in Daria's book are filled with what look like spells. One that catches my eye is:

Hair of dog, string of gum
Make this icky meal taste yum

I glance at all of the pages, which is kind of naughty, but I'm hoping it might help me work out a way to find Daria and get my suitcase back. Instead of the boring classes I have, she has things in her book like: "Broom-making workshop" and "How to groom your familiar". But then I finally see something that might help!

My poetry competition is in a place called the Grand Hotel, and it looks like the witch is going to be there at the same time. How lucky! But she's not going to the competition; she's attending a group called the **M**iraculous **a**nd **G**reat **I**deas **C**lub. It looks like she goes to it every week, which means she must be from around here. I wonder if she was coming back from a holiday?

At first, I think the group sounds a bit random, but then I realise it spells out the word "Magic". It's clearly a secret code.

This is good and bad news at the same time. Good because it means I'll be able to meet Daria and swap our suitcases back. Bad because I won't have my notebook of poems for the whole weekend, so I will have to practise them by heart.

Dad pops in a few minutes later. "Ready to go?" he says.

"I found a way to get my suitcase back," I say, and then I grab the diary. "Look!"

Mum stands next to Dad as they peer at where my finger is pointing. "It's rude to pry in other people's things, Zahra," says Mum, frowning. "But, oh, is that the same hotel?"

"Yes!" I say. "She's going to be there at the same time too. How lucky is that?"

"See?" says Dad. "No need to panic."

I smile, feeling a bit better about the situation. I'm secretly excited about the witchy things I found in Daria's diary (which I made sure not to show Mum and Dad). We head out for the evening, but I'm itching to get back and find out more.

We have a lovely time at the beach until a seagull snatches half my fishcake. But it's OK because Mum and Dad each give me a bit of theirs and take me for an ice cream too.

*

Back at the flat, I'm wearing one of Dad's T-shirts to bed. He's put my clothes in to wash overnight. But I do something VERY SILLY.

I'd been writing my poems out to practise them, and I got really annoyed because I couldn't remember the sonnet I'd written. So I decided to take a break and get some water, since my mouth had gone dry from whispering the poems aloud.

Anyway, that's not the important bit of the story. I tiptoed quietly to the kitchen to fill a glass, but when I got into my room, I had to use both hands to shut the door. Instead of putting the glass of water down, I balanced it on my arms and spilled water ALL down Dad's top. So now I'm soaking wet, and I can't wake Dad up because he gets really grumpy without a proper night's sleep.

So I do the only thing I can think of ... I change into the witch's pyjamas. To be fair, they're really nice and silky, like grown-up pyjamas. They're lilac with black cats drawn on them and jangling bells all around the cuffs and sleeves.

When I put them on, I feel different. As if I could float. It's sort of like when you sit with your head upside down for a minute before going back up the normal way. I'm all light-headed and dizzy. But that's not even the strangest part of it.

I'm finally settled in bed, nice and dry, giving up on the idea of drinking any more water. The jangling bells, I quickly discover, are a bit annoying because they make a noise whenever I move. But then I hear a faint but clear miaow coming from my window. And when I peer outside, I see a black cat on the fire escape!

It must have climbed up and up and up. I look beyond it, and there's another black cat on the step below, followed by a third and fourth.

"What's happening?!" I squeal, confused and a little afraid.

Things get even more confusing when the first cat answers, "Oh, hello, am I late for the audition?"

CHAPTER 3

A Cluster of Cats

"Audition?" I ask the cat, confused. "What audition?" But then I remember the question I *should* be asking, which is, "Why can you talk?"

The cat lets out a wheezy laugh, sort of like he's coughing up a furball. "Whatever do you mean?" he says. "We could always talk." He looks over to a kitten next to him, who also has black fur. She's smaller and fluffier, and has a small white patch on her chest.

"Mhm, yup, he's right," says the kitten. Her voice is much more high-pitched. "It's just that humans don't *listen*. Or they can't, I guess, unless they have a little help."

"Help? How?" I ask.

"Spells, enchanted items," says one of the cats from the crowd that's gathered behind. "Things like that."

I frown. "But I haven't ..." I start to say. That's when I peer down at the pyjamas I'm wearing. The cat pattern has disappeared and been replaced with stars instead. The bells all along the sleeves and cuffs are gone too. Could the pyjamas have done this? Are they enchanted? "Hang on. *What* are you auditioning for again? You never said."

"To be your familiar," says the first cat. He must have realised now that I'm very new to all of this, as he explains, "A familiar is a witch's companion. Cats are the most common, of course, but other inferior animals can be considered."

It takes me a while to process what the cat's said. "Oh, this is a misunderstanding ..." I reply. "I don't need a familiar."

"You don't?" says the first cat, surprised. "All witches need familiars. Who else will offer you advice and help you practise spells? Who else can keep you company when you have to hide who you are because humans are ignorant—"

"Ahem!" says the kitten. "You've gone on a bit of a rant again."

"Oh, sorry," says the first cat. "But you get the idea, don't you?"

"Yeees," I say, stretching the word out, because I'm not sure I do. "But you see, I'm not really a witch ..."

I let the cats into my room and wait for them to gather round my bed. Then I perch on the end and explain the situation to them.

Their ears and whiskers twitch at different points in my story.

I tell them about switching suitcases at the train station, spilling water down Dad's T-shirt and changing into Daria's pyjamas. I explain my plan to meet her at the Grand Hotel, right before I'm to perform on stage. For some reason I also tell them how nervous I am. They're very easy to talk to.

While I'd been speaking, a few of the cats climbed onto my bed and are now curled up comfortably, showing off their grooming skills. Are they already auditioning? I feel bad they've come all this way for nothing. Some of them are even balancing on one leg or chasing their tails at lightning speed.

"Do you know if Daria needs a familiar?" asks the white-chested kitten in her whispery voice. "Or maybe she already has one?"

"Oh," I say, not expecting the question. "Well, I didn't see one with her. Would Daria's familiar have been on the train?"

"Oh yes," says the first cat I'd spoken to, while a few others nod. "Witches never go *anywhere* without their familiars. They have a very strong bond. It's every witch's duty to find their familiar once they've turned thirteen."

"Daria's just turned thirteen!" I say, turning to her diary to find her birthday was this week. That could be why she went away. "Maybe she got these pyjamas to call her familiar?"

"That does make sense," the first cat says, and I'm pleased to have solved the mystery.

I wish *I* was a witch. I'm turning thirteen soon, like Daria, but Mum and Dad would never let me get a cat because they're too busy. They say I have to be more grown up before I can look after a pet myself. I'm not really sure what you have to do to be grown up besides doing the food shop every week and cleaning and cooking all the time.

Anyway, I don't say this to all the cats. Instead, I tell them exactly where the witch will be so they can audition to be her familiar instead.

"Thank you, Zahra," says the first cat, and I wonder how he knows my name because I definitely didn't tell him it.

"Would you like to practise your poems on us?" chirps up the kitten. "You mentioned you had a competition and that you were afraid of speaking to a big crowd of people ... Maybe we could help?"

I laugh and say, "But you're not people, you're cats!" And then I think that actually it might be helpful, so I do. I recite my limerick and then move on to the haiku:

Frost-tipped blade of grass
The crunch of snow underfoot
A winter greeting

When I'm done, the cats cheer so loudly I hear Mum and Dad stir. I end up having to rush them all down the fire escape. I just manage to get back into bed and pretend to be asleep before Mum and Dad pop their heads in.

"What was that?" asks Mum, fully alert. Vampire, I told you.

Dad on the other hand is more like a zombie, his hair a mess, barely opening his eyes. He yawns. "Sounded like a hundred cats were yowling in your room," he says.

"HA ... HA ..." I say, a little forced, after pretending to wake up too. "That's ridiculous. Why would that be happening?"

Dad shrugs and heads back to bed.

Mum is watching me, narrowing her eyes. VAMPIRE, see? Then I think that a vampire being the mum of a witch would be kind of cool ... "What are you wearing?" she asks.

"Oh, I spilled water on Dad's top," I say. "So I put on the witch's ... I mean the suitcase girl's pyjamas."

Mum nods, accepting this explanation. "We'll have to make sure to wash them before we give them back to her. I'm sure she'll understand. She's probably gone through your stuff too."

I hadn't thought of that. What if she's reading all of my poems? They're kind of like really bad spells but without the magic. It's so embarrassing.

But the cats seemed to like them ... Even though I couldn't recite the sonnet, as I'd forgotten it! I'm probably just tired. I'll remember it tomorrow when the day is fresh ...

After all the excitement, I drift off to sleep. I dream I'm a witch with a broom and my very own familiar to get into trouble with.

CHAPTER 4

The Forgotten Sonnet

The next morning I wake up in a daze. I wonder if I actually *did* perform my poems for a bunch of talking cats, or if it was all a strange dream.

The first clue I have that last night really happened is the witch's pyjamas I'm currently wearing. The second clue is the open window of my bedroom, which leads to the fire escape. And the third is all the random black cat hairs on my bed.

So it was real!

But it's not just excitement that washes over me, worry does too (a bit like the water I spilled on Dad's top last night). I've forgotten my sonnet! And there's no way I'll have time to learn it before the competition once I switch back with the witch.

I strain my brain by squishing my eyes and gritting my teeth and scrunching my nose. But no matter how hard I think, I can only remember about four lines of my sonnet. The problem is that sonnets are meant to be about your emotions, and when I wrote the sonnet I was really bored at school. So the poem ended up being pretty boring, which made it forgettable.

To be honest, it was my least favourite poem of the three, but I *need* it, so I look at Daria's diary/spellbook and try to find something that might help. I also find some gemstones in a little wooden box that go with the different spells.

They're charged with magic to help you cast a charm.

There's a spell that helps jog your memory – you have to jog on the spot with a ruby in your hand. I decide to try that first, but all I end up remembering is my seven times table, which is useful but not what I need right now.

In the end I decide I'm going to have to write a whole new sonnet.

"Zee?" Dad calls from the other side of my door. "I've got your clothes here, all clean. I'll leave them outside your room. Now hurry up, we're leaving in a minute. With or without you!"

I roll my eyes. Dad is so dramatic. He always says that whenever I'm late, but he's never left me behind.

"I'll be quick!" I promise because I'm keen to explore. I need to gather inspiration for my sonnet.

Once I've got my clothes on, I stand in front of the witch's suitcase and wonder if something else might be able to help.

If the pyjamas brought me a bunch of talking cats, then the cloak and boots might do something else. So, despite being worried, I decide I'm going to try them on and see what happens next, starting with the boots ...

Right now, the emotion I'd choose to write a sonnet about would be *excitement*.

CHAPTER 5

A Dancing Disaster

The boots were a bad idea. A VERY bad idea.
But I survived to tell the tale, so prepare to find
out about the most embarrassing day of my
life. Before today, the most embarrassing day
of my life was when the whole class got told off
for being too loud, so our teacher asked us all to
work silently. It was late in the afternoon and
the air was hot and I was tired, so I let out a big
yawn. Except it ended up in a BIG BURP.

Everyone gasped and looked at me while I
covered my mouth with my hands. Then they
all turned to see if the teacher had noticed,
and it was like the whole world stopped. It

didn't actually – if the world really stopped, there would be lots of natural disasters. But that's how it FELT. Somehow, the teacher hadn't noticed, but everyone made fun of me for *weeks* after and kept making burping noises when they saw me.

But today was worse than that.

Mum and Dad and I were walking along the promenade, which is a fancy word for a pavement next to the sea. It's also a word that means to go for a stroll, which is what we were doing. Loads of people seemed to be admiring my boots, which made me happy even though they weren't MY boots. And then it happened.

Someone was playing a guitar and singing in a corner next to some food stands. There were large crowds of people watching them, and Mum and Dad decided to stop and watch too. At first I was enjoying it, but then I felt a strange tingling sensation coming from my feet.

It was like getting pins and needles, and I wiggled my toes to try to get the feeling back. But then, without me controlling them, my feet started tap, tap, tapping to the music.

Mum and Dad glanced over at me and said, "What are you doing, Zee? You HATE dancing."

Which is true – I HATE dancing. We had to do a group dance in our school play once, and I was so bad at it that my teacher decided to make me a tree that everyone else had to dance around. So the fact that I suddenly could dance to a rhythm was strange.

A few other people were looking over. The music picked up its pace, and so did my feet.

They were now doing a weird two-step dance where they crossed over each other. But the magic was only in my feet, so my arms were just dangling there. I looked a bit like a puppet with its strings cut off, and by this point EVERYONE was watching.

The person who was playing and singing noticed and said, "Everyone, make way for our dancing queen!"

By this point I was DYING inside, but my feet were loving it, so they tap, tap, tapped towards the singing man. And then for ten of the

longest minutes of my life, he sang and I danced, and people clapped along. (I was crying too, but I don't think anyone noticed my face because my feet were wild.)

Afterwards, I could tell Mum and Dad didn't know if they should be proud or confused, so they made faces that looked a bit of both.

"I guess after that you won't mind reading your poems out loud, will you?" Dad said chirpily. I swear Mum was doing her best not to laugh. I should also mention that it wasn't raining, but she was carrying around an umbrella to stop the sun shining down on her. See – vampire. And she thinks *I'm* weird.

But Dad was very wrong. I am nervous about my poems, and dancing in front of everyone only made it worse. I'm also not any closer to coming up with my sonnet.

I'm going to try the witch's cloak next. But this time I'm going to wear it in private ...

CHAPTER 6

Night Flight

It's late at night and the moon is high. I can hear Mum again, secretly typing away on her laptop behind her bedroom door. Dad's probably asleep by now.

The sky is a blend of purple and blue, kissing the horizon at the sea, which looks black from here. I'm walking around the living room with the cloak wrapped around the T-shirt and shorts Dad washed for me, trying to test what sort of magic will come from it.

Down on the street below, there are only a few people dotted around – a nurse on their way to work, someone walking a dog, and someone else waiting for a bus. The woman waiting for the bus is wearing a bright dress with a matching beret. A sudden gust of wind swoops the beret off her head, and it lands on next door's balcony. The woman looks really upset, and I can see her bus is about to arrive.

I have no idea what makes me do it, but I open the living-room window and lean over the balcony.

"I can reach your beret, don't worry!" I call down to the woman.

Her eyes widen, and she looks frightened. "No, don't," she says. "You'll hurt yourself."

But I ignore her and lean forward even more. I can squeeze my hand through the bars of the other balcony. I'm a few centimetres away from the beret and lean over just a little bit more when ... *CRACK*.

The bar of the balcony I'm on snaps off. I feel myself fall forward, head-first towards the pavement below.

The beret woman screams, but things move too fast for me to make a sound. Then I feel the same tingly sensation of magic, but this time in my shoulders instead of my feet. Just as I'm about to slam into the ground, I swoop back up and hover in the air like a hummingbird. The cloak is trailing behind me, acting like wings.

The woman's screaming face has frozen into a look of wonder.

It takes me a few moments to realise that I can fly in the way that you might swim. So I do a little doggy paddle towards the hat (not the most elegant, but it works). I return it to the woman just in time as her bus arrives.

While the moon is high, I decide I'm going to go on an adventure!

*

I fly straight towards the beach, swooping past the pebbles until I reach the ocean. I pause for a moment, hovering on the spot, then fly towards the windmills that break up the horizon.

I'm astounded by how bright it is out here with the stars winking down at me. The waves lap beneath me as I fly just above the water.

The further I go, the darker the water gets, and I feel a bit scared when I imagine what lies beneath the surface.

After a while, the town behind me looks like a miniature toy set. I don't want to lose sight of it completely, so I loop round and round for a while, then make my way back. Bravely, I let my hand touch the surface of the ocean and it's

ice cold. The waves reach up for me as I reach out for them, as if they want to pull me under.

I'm feeling more confident with my newfound wings, so I walk across the ocean. My cloak stops me from sinking into the depths of it. And I promise myself to never forget what this magical moment feels like.

Once I get back home, I set my wet shoes on the radiator to dry. I keep the cloak on, the smell of the sea woven into it, as I write my new sonnet:

The Night

The night is full of shadows,
*   sparking fear,*
I hide beneath the covers on
*   my bed,*
I hope that the scraping sounds
*   I can hear,*
Aren't hungry monsters that
*   need to be fed.*

The night is filled with nightmares
and with woe,

With worries that swirl and whirl
all around.

I'm trapped in my bed with
nowhere to go,

I hope that by morning, light will
be found.

But past my window, a star
sparkles bright,

I put on a cloak and stand on
the sill.

A gust of wind throws me into
the night,

I fly, with wings, my fear turning
to thrill.

I glide through the sky while the
world is in slumber,

I fly through the night; all I feel
now is wonder.

CHAPTER 7

A Useful Spell

It's the morning of the competition and I feel SICK with nerves. My stomach is doing somersaults the way I did in the sky when I wore the cloak. The good thing is I remember all three poems, even the sonnet. I only wrote it last night, but it was all so exciting that the words stuck to my brain like papier mâché on a balloon.

The bad thing is I'm still nervous about having to read my poems out in front of HUNDREDS of people. I feel like this even after practising in front of the cats and dancing in front of a bunch of strangers.

Dad is insisting I have a proper energising breakfast, so he said I'm not allowed pancakes or French toast (my favourites). Instead, he is making me have icky porridge with raisins in it. Even Mum doesn't seem pleased to eat it.

She takes her seat at the table and pulls a face, saying to Dad, "I'm wondering, now, why I ever married you ..." She's drinking "cranberry juice", which I'm certain is actually blood.

If we're going with my theory that Mum is a vampire, then I'm starting to wonder if Dad *is* a zombie. I have evidence for this:

1.) He sleeps a lot. (I don't know if zombies sleep a lot, but they always shuffle around like they're really tired.)

2.) Dad makes funny noises in the morning when he's trying to get up, which sound like zombie growls. It's especially funny when I pull the curtains open and let the sunlight in. But actually, sunlight is more of a vampire thing ...

3.) DAD EATS BRAINS. OK, so technically not brains, but the porridge Dad has plopped in front of me looks very much like brains. It's a little too dry, and the raisins look like mouse poop.

I'm going to need something magical to help me get through breakfast. The witch's things are all packed neatly in her suitcase, ready to return to her when we arrive at the hotel. Dad washed her PJs, and I've not touched anything else besides the cloak and boots. But there's this really pretty brooch in the shape of a dragonfly with gems studded all over it ...

No – I'm not going to risk trying the brooch when I'm not sure what it will do. And anyway, there's a spell I remember looking at when I first found Daria's diary.

Dad's busy making some coffee and Mum is adding spoonfuls of sugar to her porridge to try and make it taste nice (it won't), meaning I can carry out my plan. In my left hand I'm holding an opal from the wooden box in Daria's suitcase, while my right hand hovers over the food. And then I recite the words from the spell as quietly as I can:

Hair of dog, string of gum
Make this icky meal taste yum

"Right!" Dad says, taking his seat at the table with his mug. "Eat up!"

Mum and I look at each other and sigh. I take a bite.

I widen my eyes. "OH MY GOODNESS!" I say, with my mouth full.

Dad looks up, a little alarmed. "What's wrong? Did I not mix the porridge up properly? Zee, just spit it out if—"

"No," I say, swallowing my bite. It seeps down my throat in the most satisfying way because the porridge and raisins taste like cookie dough and chocolate chips. "It's DELICIOUS!"

Mum looks at me like I've just turned into a lizard. But Dad looks really pleased.

"Well, thank you, Zee," Dad says. "I'm glad you like it. I added a top-secret ingredient ..." He pauses. "It's cinnamon. Gives it a zing!"

I'm glad I've made Dad happy. And *I'm* happy because I'm eating my favourite dessert in the whole world.

I'm still nervous about later on, but I feel energised, just like Dad promised.

CHAPTER 8

Meeting a Witch

The Grand Hotel is beautiful. It's a big old building that looks a bit like a palace, and it has a swivelly door that spins round to let you inside. I'm not wearing any of the witch's clothes in case something goes horribly wrong, but I have her suitcase with me and her diary in my hand so I can double-check what room the MAGIC meeting is in.

I'm supposed to recite my poems in forty-five minutes, which means I need to be backstage in half an hour. I feel ready, I think, which surprises me. But I'm still nervous.

The inside of the building is even more beautiful than the front, with marble floors and wood-panelled walls. There's a big circular desk in the middle of the entryway with three people waiting to help you find what you're looking for. I ask about the Miraculous and Great Ideas Club, and they point me down one of the many maze-like hallways.

"Are you *sure* you want to go on your own?" Dad asks anxiously. I've told him he has to go and watch all of the other performances to tell me how they've done. Mum's gone ahead to save them both a good seat.

"*Yes*," I say for the hundredth time. I don't really want the witch to see me with my dad. I remember how confident she seemed getting the train on her own, and I want to be the same.

Finally, Dad lets me go and I wander the halls, quickly forgetting the instructions the person at the desk gave me. Luckily, there's someone familiar headed in the right direction. Or should I say *a* familiar.

"Oh, hello!" I say, jogging up to the kitten with the white chest. The one with the soft whispery voice.

She turns to me, looking surprised, but maybe it's just because she has these big orange eyes. "Ah, you made it then?" the kitten asks.

I nod. "So did you," I say. "Good luck with your audition!"

She peeks into the room first and curls her ears back. "The others are here too," the kitten says. "I don't stand a chance against all of them."

I frown. "I'm sure you do!" I say, wishing I could take her home myself. Then I realise something. "Why can I understand you? I haven't got any witch's clothes on."

The kitten thinks about this for a moment. "Maybe some of the magic has rubbed off on you? From when you last used it?"

That makes sense. I suppose the magic will disappear in the end and I won't hear cats speak any more. The thought makes me sad. I wish the kitten luck again before she leaves.

"Good luck to you too," she says. "For your competition!" And then she disappears inside the room.

"Oh!" a surprised voice says from behind me a few moments later. I turn to see the witch from the train. Daria. "Is that my suitcase?"

"Yes!" I say, holding it out to her. Then I explain. "I saw you were going to be here today, and I have a poetry competition in just ..." I glance at the clock and see I've only got about twenty minutes until I need to get backstage. "About half an hour."

Daria looks impressed by what I've told her, which makes me feel warm and fuzzy inside. "Well, good luck!" she says. "Hang on, I'll get your suitcase ..."

"Oh, don't worry ..." I say, thinking she's about to rush back home to go and get it. But of course, she's a witch.

Daria takes one of the gemstones from her suitcase and recites a quick spell. In the blink of an eye my suitcase has appeared and we trade back. She asks me what I want to wear for the competition, as I mention I'll need to change quickly.

"Don't worry, I can do that for you." Daria grabs another gemstone and recites another spell. Suddenly, the outfit I had picked for the competition is on my body, freshly ironed. "It feels good to be using magic again," she says.

I smile. "If I was a witch, I'd use magic every day!"

Daria laughs. "I do! But living like you for a weekend was fun too. Your clothes are really cool. I *love* your shoes, especially."

I grin. "Thank you. But I hope you don't mind that I wore some of your clothes? And I used some spells too. One of them made my dad's food taste better ..."

I worry for a moment that Daria will be annoyed, but she just laughs.

"You can keep my shoes," I offer, as a way of thanking her. "If you like them so much?"

Daria widens her eyes. "Really? That would be so cool. It means we'd be able to keep in touch too, because I'll have something of yours."

I laugh now. "Don't you have, like, a phone or a laptop?" I ask.

Daria scrunches up her face. "The frequency of things like that sort of messes with the magic. But anyway, *you'll* also need something of mine. Is there anything you'd like in particular?"

I think about the pyjamas, but I'm not sure I want to summon hundreds of cats to my room again. The boots are a definite no after embarrassing me in public. The cloak is cool, but I doubt Mum and Dad would let me fly regularly once they found out about it. I shrug and say, "You decide!"

Daria grins. "You have a poetry competition in a minute, right? I have just the thing ..."

CHAPTER 9

The Poetry Competition

I make it backstage just in time, and my nerves catch up with me all at once. There are a bunch of people, all my age, from all over the country. A few look as nervous as I am, and the one who's just been up to read their poems is crying quietly in the corner. It doesn't help me feel better AT ALL.

I'm glad to be back in my clothes, which feel familiar and safe, but I now also have the witch's brooch pinned to the collar of my dress. It's shaped like a dragonfly, with gems making up its body and wings.

The brooch shimmers orange and blue in the light and something about it makes me feel a bit less afraid. I don't know what magic it does, but Daria promised me the brooch wouldn't embarrass me like the shoes did and that it'll help. She wanted it to be a surprise, though ...

"You're up!" a woman with a headset and clipboard says to me, gently ushering me to the side of the stage.

As I walk out, it feels like everything is happening in slow motion. Hundreds of people are seated on chairs in front of me, watching my every move.

There's a podium and microphone. When I step up to it, the microphone gives out a sharp squeaking noise, which makes me jump and a few people in the audience gasp.

This isn't going well so far.

I clear my throat and the sounds blasts across the room. Oh dear.

I'm not really looking at everyone, but my teacher told me I should try to. She said I should move my gaze across the room so I'm not just staring at one person.

I introduce myself and my school, in a voice that's a little shaky from the nerves. I look out into the audience, and I see Mum and Dad, front row with the other parents, smiling at me. Their familiar faces in a sea of strangers helps calm me.

Then the weird, tingling sensation happens as the magic Daria promised comes to life.

All of the scary adults in the audience in front of me transform. Now they're wearing silly outfits like flippers and swimming goggles, or cat ears and fluffy tails.

Something about seeing them like this makes me grin, and I recite my poems confidently and clearly, exactly how I practised.

When I'm done, the crowd cheers, and when I go backstage, I don't want to cry or throw up – I want to buzz around with excitement!

Then it's time for the announcements from the judge:

"Our third-place winner, for her wonderfully *magical* poems, is ... Zahra!"

Everyone claps politely, except Mum and Dad – they give me a standing ovation while cheering loudly. And because my brooch is still on, they're wearing fruit costumes. Mum is a banana and Dad is a bunch of grapes.

I haven't won first place and a £500 voucher for my school, but I do get a medal. What's even better is that I'm told my sonnet has been selected to be published in a book of poems next year! The girl who I saw crying is declared the winner, and I'm glad because her sad tears turn to happy ones.

"Let's celebrate!" Dad says when we leave through the swivelly doors again. "I found a lovely little dessert shop that does your favourite ... cookie dough and chocolate chips!"

Dad doesn't know I already secretly ate that for breakfast, so I get to have it all over again. Turns out, this has been the best weekend EVER.

CHAPTER 10

When Magic Follows You Home

We've been back home for a few weeks now, and Daria and I have kept in touch. Right now, a magically projected version of her is lounging on my bed. I'm telling her about school and how I spent my thirteenth birthday, and she's telling me more about what it's like to be a witch.

Mum and Dad enjoyed our weekend away so much we're going to visit the same town again in the summer holidays, but for a whole week. And Daria has promised to show me lots more magic.

I use the brooch now whenever I'm feeling worried, like during a school exam or if I have to go to the dentist. It makes everything feel a little less scary and a lot more silly. Even Mum and Dad have noticed how confident I've been.

While Daria and I are chatting, Dad calls me from downstairs. He sounds a bit worried, so I rush down, hopping two steps at a time.

"What's wrong?" I ask, out of breath from running.

Dad's standing by the open door of the house. "Come here!"

I do, and I see the little kitten with the white chest sitting on the doorstep. "What are *you* doing here?" I ask. I quickly realise that might sound confusing to Dad, but he doesn't seem to suspect anything.

"I know," Dad says. "This kitten has just been sitting there, watching us. I've not seen her around before, and she hasn't got a collar ..."

The kitten responds, but of course Dad doesn't hear her. "I want to be your familiar!" she explains. "You were so wonderful and kind, and I know you're not a full witch, but I don't care. Please, may I?"

I bite my lip, wanting to reply directly to the kitten, but of course I can't because Dad's standing right there. So instead I say, "Can we keep her? She's so sweet and deserves the best home ever, which I think we could give her."

I expect Dad to say a big NO, but in fact he says, "Only if she doesn't have another owner *and* your mum says yes. Why don't you go and get her? I'll watch the kitten."

I rush into the living room, where Mum was busy working earlier, and gasp. Mum is ASLEEP on the sofa. I guess she isn't a vampire after all. After I wake her, Dad and I show her the kitten, and Mum says, "As long as you promise to clean up her poop and feed her—"

"Yes, yes, yes!" I say, hopping up and down.

So now, like a proper witch, I have a familiar and a little magical brooch. Daria's life seems pretty cool, but I think that's just enough magic for me.